Baiting Hollow

A Pastel Summer

Patricia Clark Smith

Order this book online at www.trafford.com
or email orders@trafford.com

Most Trafford titles are also available at major online book retailers.

Print information available on the last page.

ISBN: 978-1-4907-6709-3 (sc)
ISBN: 978-1-4907-6708-6 (e)

Library of Congress Control Number: 2015918801

Trafford rev.   11/11/2015

 www.trafford.com

North America & international
toll-free: 1 888 232 4444 (USA & Canada)
fax: 812 355 4082

Dedicated with love, to my beautiful Aunt Clare

for her kindness, friendship, faith and love.

B aiting Hollow beach has always held the possibility of the romantic. Brigid and Barbara loved their relatives' stories from the 1930's and 1940's of the fun they had with beach friends, soldiers patrolling the beach, and just hanging out with family and friends. There were stories of gathering for picnics, beach parties, holy day celebrations, and meeting for a swim after work on a hot summer evening.

Brigid and Barbara had their own childhood memories of summers at the Twomey family farm in Calverton, Long Island, and their Aunt Agatha and Uncle Al Meyer's Baiting Hollow bungalow three miles up the road from the family farm. Generations of Baiting Hollow families met, played on the beach, swam to the raft, walked to the creek, sat together around bonfires at night and became life-long friends. Beach kids attended college, moved away, went off to war, or answered calls to religious life. Some fell in love, married, and raised the next generation of beach kids.

It was Sunday, July 10, 2011. Barbara, now professor at Central Connecticut State University, and Brigid, retired elementary school principal, had waited all year to return to Baiting Hollow beach, to the mercottage they had rented for the past two summers. Their 2009 and 2010 two week vacations were wonderful. This summer would be even more fun, because Aunt Clare was staying with them! The little one room mercottage would be home to the three mermaids for two weeks.

Barbara and Brigid sat in a booth on the Bridgeport ferry enjoying their morning coffee while gazing out the window. Long Island Sound was still, a grey-blue stillness under the hazy morning sky. It felt as though they were passing through time and space from their busy and sometimes hectic lives in Connecticut to their vacation home on Long Island. They talked about movies like *Shangri-la* and *Brigadoon*, mysterious wonderful places just on the other side of our senses, which had some similarity to, but could not compare with the beauty and enchantment of Baiting Hollow.

Aunt Clare drove from East Islip, Long Island and met Barbara and Brigid at Applebee's restaurant in Riverhead. They had salads for lunch and caught up on news about family before going to Baiting Hollow.

Driving down Edward's Avenue, Barbara stopped the car at the top of the hill to admire the view of Baiting Hollow: the cliffs, water, gigantic boulders at the foot of the cliffs, cottages, sky, jetties, and beach. They paused for a few minutes, inhaled, and continued down the beach road to the back of the mercottage.

Aunt Clare, Barbara, and Brigid brought their suitcases, tote bags, and sleeping bags into the cottage and discussed sleeping arrangements. Barbara had the bunk bed, Aunt Clare would sleep on the bed, and Brigid had a cot from home.

The beach was magnificent: clean, breezy, full of sunshine. Ah, just as they had remembered. After taking in the views of the beach, putting their toes in the water, and arranging their belongings in the bungalow, it was time to go grocery shopping. They discussed ideas for meals and made a grocery list. Aunt Clare said she would like to stay at the cottage, so Barbara and Brigid went to the store.

When they returned to the bungalow, they found Aunt Clare, a vision of loveliness and peace, on the back deck in her red and white bathing suit sitting in a wicker chair and reading her book. So beautiful!

That evening around 8:00 PM, Barbara, Aunt Clare and Brigid set three sand chairs on the beach and relaxed, ready to enjoy the sunset. Their 2011 two week summer vacation in Baiting Hollow had begun.

Monday morning, they woke up to a magnificent sunrise. Aunt Clare made the coffee while Barbara and Brigid set up three beach umbrellas and sand chairs just above the high tide line. Around 10:30 AM, Barbara,

Brigid, and Aunt Clare had their bathing suits, suntan lotion, and hats on and carried their sunglasses, beach towels, water bottles, and books down to the beach. They decided to go for a swim right away. The water was crystal clear, calm, and a little chilly.

That afternoon, Aunt Clare reminisced about harvesting mussels in the jetties at the east end of the beach, bringing them back to Aunt Agatha's bungalow, and having them for dinner. The three discussed their likes and dislikes of mussels, whether the water was clean and safe, and the fact that mussels were famine food during the nineteenth century potato famine in Ireland. Brigid said there were mussels on the third jetty right in front of the mercottage. She ran up to the bungalow to get three plastic bags to hold the mussels they planned to harvest.

Aunt Clare cleaned the mussels, cooked them, and served them with melted butter for dinner that evening. Barbara made a delicious salad for dinner, and Brigid washed and served strawberries for dessert. The table was set with a bouquet of wildflowers they picked on their walk to the creek that afternoon.

Brigid woke up Tuesday morning and looked around the quiet bungalow, no Barbara and no Aunt Clare. They were not in the bathroom or kitchen. She noticed two chairs were missing, heard the soft hum of voices, looked out on the deck and found them sitting on the side of the bungalow. Brigid said, "Good morning", then went inside to pour her coffee, and joined them on the deck. Aunt Clare was sharing her manuscript for her story, *Growing up Twomey*, with Barbara. She asked if Barbara and Brigid would read it with her one day and offer insights and comments. They said, "We'd love to."

That afternoon, the sky grew dark, the water turned blue-green, and a strong wind blew across the beach. Later they learned that type of weather is called a *sheer*.

That evening Peter Shilling, next door neighbor, invited the three mermaids to come to his bungalow for a glass of wine. They accepted his invitation. Wine, conversation, stories, memories, laughter filled the bungalow. Peter shared two statements he believed, "Women are just as screwed up as men. I don't know anything about women." He told a story about how he met his wife. She was the girlfriend of a buddy of his. He traded his car for a date with his friend's girlfriend. They were later married. Peter shared stories about his Uncle Frederick Shilling.

Aunt Clare said she knew his parents, Nancy and Peter Shilling. "Theirs was a great love story of Baiting Hollow," Aunt Clare remembered.

Then Aunt Clare, Barbara, and Brigid shared their wishes for vacation. Barbara wished for her brother, Eddie, to be safe and well. Brigid wished for a peaceful, happy vacation. Aunt Clare wished to gather mussels again, cook them, and eat them.

Barbara wondered how many waves hit the shore in Baiting Hollow since the glaciers receded. Brigid thought it might be more or less than the national debt. Peter said, "Less!" and laughed. He started to estimate by listening to the waves while watching the clock: 16 waves per minute X 60 minutes X 24 hours a day X 365 days in a year X 50,000 years…He then said he'd have to take more data samples, not just one.

Brigid wondered how the tide shifted directions. Was there an energy shift? Peter explained the moon's pull.

Peter walked the ladies home that evening. He said there had been a rainbow in the east that afternoon after the storm sheer.

Wednesday morning was cool and windy with choppy waves on the sound. The water was stirred up with seaweed from yesterday's storm. Aunt Clare, Barbara, and Brigid had their coffee and breakfast. They sat on the deck and talked about the fun they had the night before at Peter Shilling's bungalow, and that he was a gentleman for walking them home.

The three mermaids had plans to meet relatives (Patsy, Dottie, and Henry and Pat) at the Cooperage for lunch that day. It would be so nice to see everyone. During lunch Henry talked about going to sporting events with his grandson, Stephen. Pat said their granddaughter, Savannah, was going into second grade. Patsy shared that her granddaughter was 14 years old and an accomplished dancer with the American Ballet in New York. Dottie told us that Peter Shilling scared her to death when they were kids. They were at the raft. He kept dunking her. She said she felt like she was drowning.

After lunch Aunt Clare asked Barbara to drive to Riverhead, so she could show Brigid and her where the Kaelin home was in Riverhead. Grandma Margaret J. Kaelin Twomey, her mother, grew up there. Barbara then drove to Saint John's Cemetery where they visited Aunt Clare's husband's (Uncle Frank) grave and the Twomey and Kaelin graves. Aunt Clare cleaned the geraniums Patsy had planted that spring.

When they arrived back at the bungalow, the sky was blue, sunny, and breezy. It was low tide. Aunt Clare and Barbara went for a walk to the creek. They stopped on the way and talked with Laurie Erickson sitting on the jetty.

Brigid decided to work on the Twomey and Kaelin family trees which she was making for Christmas presents for her family. Then she read an article in *Dan's Magazine* on "Turtle Migration" by Dan Rattiner.

At 6:30 PM, Brigid brought the sand chairs down to the beach for sunset. Laurie Erickson waved and said, "Hello." Aunt Clare and Barbara returned from their walk with a surprise. They reported they saw a large red and purple jellyfish in the creek. They also said that, *Will you marry me?* was written with stones in the sand dune near the creek. "How very romantic," Brigid whispered. Baiting Hollow is always full of surprises.

Laurie took a picture of Aunt Clare, Barbara, and Brigid from her deck. Then she came to sit with them and watch the sunset. Bobby and Marcy Edwards came to visit with their chairs and set them on the beach. Peter and his girl friend, Madi, came and joined everyone.

The sunset was spectacular. The sky and sound were a pastel wash of pink, orange, red, and purple. As the sun set and the colors faded, a great full moon appeared.

Every star was shining. The lights on the Connecticut shore were sparkling. It was a beautiful evening full of stories, teasing, and laughter.

Aunt Clare shared the great love story of Peter Shilling's parents' meeting in Baiting Hollow. Then, Brigid shared the story of her mother's and father's meeting at a party one night and how he proposed to her that evening. They were married three months later.

Barbara shared Dottie's story about Peter's dunking her. Peter denied it and tried to figure out who she might have been thinking of.

When the conversation quieted, Bobby pointed to Peter and Madi and asked, "Who are the speeders? There are little kids running around. Slow down." Peter and Madi nodded in agreement. Brigid and Barbara always considered Bobby Edwards, the guardian of Baiting Hollow. They admired him for speaking to Peter and Madi about speeding on the dirt beach road.

On Thursday, Brigid awoke to Aunt Clare's whispering to Barbara that she was driving home to East

Islip this morning to copy the second half of her story. Her granddaughter, Alyssa, was visiting after work, so Aunt Clare would be back before sunset.

It was a magnificent day: blue sky, calm water, gentle waves lapping the shore, soft breezes. Brigid wondered what the day would bring.

Barbara and Brigid sat on the deck with their morning coffee admiring their precious Baiting Hollow. Peter Shilling stopped by to say they'd have a bonfire tonight. The girls said they'd be there. Then, he noticed his brother, "Oh, there's Roger and Sue walking back from the creek with their Doberman." Up and over the jetty the dog led with Sue holding on to the chain leash. Peter walked down to meet them.

After Peter left, there was a knock at the back door. It was Dottie and her husband, Frannie. They came with a tray of fresh fluke Frannie caught yesterday while fishing at Shinnecock on the south fork of Long Island. Frannie had cleaned them, so they were ready to cook for their dinner.

Dottie said she was thinking about *the dunker* story and realized it wasn't Peter Shilling. It was Peter Cummings who was the dunker.

When they left, Barbara set up the three beach umbrellas in the sand. Brigid brought the sand chairs down to the beach. Worried about the two jellyfish sightings, they brought meat tenderizer down in their beach bag just in case they were stung.

The tide was coming up so Barbara and Brigid decided to go for a swim. The water was clean with no sign of jelly fish. They said a little prayer to the Blessed Mother to keep the jelly fish away, dove in, swam back and forth, and floated around for awhile. Then they rested in the sand chairs under their umbrellas. Puffy white clouds dotted the northern Connecticut horizon and floated south and over the sound. A sailboat or two glided by in the distance, seagulls were flying and diving. There was a soft breeze. "Mmm, heavenly," thought Barbara.

Bobby Edwards, walking down the beach, came and sat with Brigid and Barbara for a little visit. He said he had a nice swim down by the creek and that the water here was cleaner than there. He told us that Marcy had fallen on her way back home last night and scraped her leg. She hit her head and her knee, but she'll be alright. "Ouch!" Barbara and Brigid said with a wince.

Laurie stopped by to say, "Hello."

A blimp floated by advertizing Hanger Vodka.

Peter Shilling hollered from the deck of his bungalow, "Are you hoping they'll land?" They all laughed.

A few minutes later Peter was in the water with his red bathing cap. They watched him swim to the creek (about a half mile), back to the jetty, back to the creek, back to the jetty, and then walk up the beach to his bungalow. The girls decided he was training for his triathlon he told them about Tuesday night. Laurie had to go make dinner for her family and said, "Good bye."

As Barbara and Brigid rested and read, a middle aged couple walking down the beach, stopped to talk. They mentioned they were the present owners of the Twomey farmhouse. Barbara told them that her mother, Lillian, was one of the Twomeys, and her sister, their Aunt Clare, was staying with them. The wife explained that they loved the house and had planned to live there forever. But, they just learned that the husband's job might be transferred down south, and they might have to sell. They asked Barbara and Brigid not to mention it to anybody before they knew for sure. Barbara asked if she could look at it before going back to Connecticut, and they agreed. "Stop in anytime." They gave Barbara their phone number and continued their walk.

When they left, Barbara and Brigid sat in silence for a few minutes. Then Barbara said, "Can you imagine it, Brigid? Maybe I could buy the Twomey farmhouse. I've always wanted to live on Long Island when I retire. Maybe this is my chance. I could live in my apartment in Connecticut Monday through Friday and leave

Friday afternoon to spend weekends and vacations on Long Island. When I retire, I would live on Long Island permanently."

Brigid took a deep breath and exhaled. She said, "It is all very exciting, but is it possible?"

Barbara looked down at the sand, paused, and then looked up and said, "I want to go look at it now and talk with them. Will you stay here in case Aunt Clare comes home? I'll be right back."

"O.K.," Brigid agreed.

Barbara gathered her beach towel, book, hat, glasses, and lotion. Brigid said, "I'll take care of the chairs and umbrellas."

"Thank you, Brigid," Barbara said. She ran up to the cottage to shower and change. Barbara hollered back over her shoulder, "Wish me luck, cross your fingers, pray for me!"

"I will," Brigid hollered back.

Brigid sat staring at the book on her lap in a daze. "What just happened?" she thought. "Is it possible? Is it possible that Barbara could buy the Twomey farmhouse? It would be a dream come true."

Brigid closed her eyes and was transported back to 1960. She saw herself sitting at the farmhouse kitchen table with Aunt Mame standing by the stove in her blue Bermuda shorts, blue and pink plaid blouse, black tie shoes, white ankle socks, and yellow calico apron. Her short curly white hair framed her face (blue eyes, fair skin with freckles, pink lipstick, glasses, and a beautiful smile). Uncle Bud, Uncle David, Uncle Johnny, Uncle Chris, Sonny, Bobby, Richie, Uncle Joe and Joey came in the kitchen door for their 10:00 morning coffee break with Mame. She poured them all a cup of coffee. They each served themselves cream and sugar from the table. Then Mame went into the pantry and brought out a platter of powdered sugar donuts she made that morning.

Brigid could almost smell Aunt Mame's donuts in her daydream. She could see all her uncles' biting into them and almost hear their talking and laughter. After their morning coffee and donuts, Uncle Johnny stood up, thanked Mame, grabbed his hat, and walked out the door heading back to work on the farm. The other uncles and cousins stood up too, thanked Mame, and headed out the door behind Johnny.

Brigid was startled out of her delightful day dream by a cold wave tickling her feet. The water was rough now, high waves and white caps on the sound. So, Brigid moved the chairs and umbrellas up the beach. Then she decided to go for another swim. She walked over the small stones and into the water ankle deep. Brrr, it was icy cold. A large wave hit her legs and splashed cold salty water all over her.

Brigid took a deep breath, put her hands on her hips, and looked to the east and then to the west. Not a soul on the beach. She couldn't believe it. Her beach which she painted pictures of, wrote poems about, dreamed about all winter, and held in a special place in her heart was all hers today. She closed her eyes and tried to imprint in her mind the views of the cliffs, sky, and sea, so it would be with her always.

As she opened her eyes she noticed the bungalows along the beach, little cottages on stilts probably built between 1930 and 1940. They were summer homes of her friends and relatives. Their spirits seemed present that day to Brigid. How she longed to see them all one more time.

Brigid turned facing the sound, took two or three leaps through the water, and dove in. Surrounded by the icy salt water, Brigid felt alive. She opened her eyes and saw the sun's golden rays pierce the blue-green underwater world. Four long slow breast strokes pulled her along as she glided past colored stones, sea shells, minnows, and bits of seaweed.

Brigid surfaced, dove back under, glided along, and surfaced again. She swam to the far jetty, turned and swam back. When she stood up, she was happy to see Barbara standing on the deck of the mercottage waving, "I'm going to put on my suit, and I'll be right there."

Brigid decided to swim back to the far jetty while waiting for her sister. She wondered what news Barbara had from her visit to the farmhouse.

As she swam back to the third jetty she noticed the late afternoon sun descending in the sky. "It must be around 4:30 or 5:00," she thought to herself.

Barbara came down to the water, ran right in, and dove under. After several strokes she stopped and wiped the water from her face.

"Well?" asked Brigid. "I've been waiting."

Barbara swam over to Brigid, stood up, and said, "The Twomey farmhouse is beautiful. The wife said she'd phone me if and when they decided to sell. The price is right at the top of the range I've been thinking of."

Brigid gave Barbara a big hug and they collapsed in the water. "Let's go up on the beach, and I'll tell you all about it," Barbara suggested.

Aunt Clare arrived at the mercottage around 6:00 PM. She brought groceries, wine, her manuscript, and a few personal things from home. Brigid decided to set the table while Barbara made dinner: steamed vegetables and broiled fluke with pepper and lemon juice.

They were enjoying a bowl of strawberries for dessert when there was a knock at the back door. Alyssa, Aunt Clare's granddaughter, came for a visit. She just finished her freshman year of college and was working at the Riverhead Aquarium for the summer. She told about college life, summer work, and her little dog. She shared pictures of her little dog.

Around 8:00 PM everyone went outside to see the sunset and enjoy the bonfire. Madi and Peter joined them on the beach. The sunset was spectacular. Peachy pink clouds filled the sky, followed by a full moon which lit the night sky and beach like mid-day.

Sitting together, enjoying the peace and beauty of Baiting Hollow, Aunt Clare asked if anyone would like a glass of wine. It was unanimous. So, Brigid and Barbara went up to the bungalow and brought glasses and wine for everyone.

The sunset passed and in the gentle evening talk, a debate emerged about the causes of school failure which was basically unresolved. Everyone did agree on the need for good teachers.

Around 10:30 PM everyone said good night and put the sand chairs back by the deck until tomorrow.

Friday they woke to a beautiful morning. The water was calm, sun shining, blue sky, and a soft breeze. After coffee and morning chores (sweep the sand out of the bungalow and deck, water the plants, tidy the cottage, and put the garbage out), Barbara set up the beach chairs and umbrellas. Around noon they went for a swim. It was a quiet dreamy day on the beach.

That night Barbara made a delicious salad with the cold fish left over from last night's dinner. After dinner, Barbara, Brigid, and Aunt Clare took a little walk to the creek to gather wild flowers for a bouquet for Marcy Edwards. Then they walked to the Edward's bungalow, knocked on the door, and Bobby welcomed them in.

Bobby, Marcy, their son, Bobby Jr., and his wife were sitting on the front porch.

Marcy told about her walk home the other night and how she tripped and fell in front of their bungalow. Brigid, Bobby Jr., and Barbara told stories about the fun they had as kids on the beach years ago. Bobby, Marcy, and Aunt Clare talked about the families who used to have cottages in Baiting Hollow and where they are now. Marcy invited everyone to the kitchen for cinnamon nut coffee cake she baked that morning and pink lemonade. Marcy said the coffee cake recipe was from Mrs. Dottie McGrath, a Baiting Hollow neighbor. She gave a copy to Barbara, Brigid, and Aunt Clare. It was a perfect summer evening with friends.

The second week of vacation was better than the first. Aunt Clare gathered and cleaned mussels for several dinners with fresh corn-on-the-cob she bought at the farm stand on Sound Avenue. Tuesday evening cousin Henry and his wife, Pat, visited. Wednesday afternoon, Leo and Debbie, Aunt Clare's son and daughter-in-law, visited. Patsy visited on the beach Thursday and had a swim. Sonny and Pat Harrison's daughter, Kerry, visited, too. Every evening before going to bed, they said the Rosary together. Sunrises were magnificent, second only to the masterpiece enjoyed every evening at sunset.

The bungalow was surrounded by nature: marsh birds (heron, egret, seagulls, terns, piping plovers), insects (flies, bumble bees, dragonflies, butterflies), reptiles (snakes, frogs), mammals (chipmunks, rabbits, mice) on the land and minnows, jelly fish, and little crabs in the water. Although being initially startled by the discovery of the snake and frog on the deck, the girls and Mother Nature lived peacefully side-by-side.

It was Saturday, July 23, 2011, a 105 degree summer day. Brigid, Barbara, and Aunt Clare, knowing they would be going home tomorrow, decided to go to 5:00 PM Mass at Saint John's Church in Riverhead and then visit their ancestors buried in the Church cemetery. They said prayers at the graves, dead-headed the geraniums, and remembered their dear relatives. Aunt Clare shared stories about the relationships of the Twomeys, Kaelins, Jewetts, and other relatives. Aunt Clare, Barbara, and Brigid said a special prayer at Uncle Frank's grave. By 6:15 PM they left the cemetery for their 6:30 PM reservations at *Jerry and the Mermaid* restaurant in Riverhead.

Walking back to the mercottage that evening, the cottages along the beach road were silhouetted by a beautiful sunset: pink, purple, orange with gold trimmed puffy clouds. Barbara unlocked the cottage door, and they went in.

The bungalow felt like an oven, so Barbara and Brigid opened the shutters to let in the cool night air. Aunt Clare suggested they sit outside on the front deck. The stars were out, and tiny lights flickered on the Connecticut horizon. High tide and a gentle breeze made it a beautiful evening.

Suddenly, fireworks filled the sky: red, green, yellow lights shot off the beach and cliffs exploding over the dark waters of Long Island Sound. In the darkness they could hear, "Ooh," "Ah," "Wow," and clapping up and down the beach.

When the fireworks were over, the beach was quiet again. Barbara, Aunt Clare, and Brigid enjoyed the peace of their beautiful beach. "There is a bonfire in front of the Shilling's bungalow," Barbara noticed.

"There are bonfires in front of the Erickson's and the Tallmadge's bungalows, too," Brigid pointed out.

Barbara stood up and looked to the east, "A bonfire in front of the Lewan's bungalow and one in front of Steve and Tina's bungalow."

"Five bonfires on the beach, oh my," Aunt Clare exclaimed.

"Why, what does it mean?" Barbara asked.

"It means the seanchai is coming," answered Aunt Clare.

"Who is the seanchai?" Barbara and Brigid asked.

"The storyteller," explained Aunt Clare. "Remember last night when we visited Bobby and Marcy Edwards, Bobby said Captain Kevin O'Connell had visited just before we came to visit. He has become Baiting Hollow's storyteller. Captain O'Connell travels the world; sailing the seas from Atlantic to Pacific. Everyone heard he visited the Edwards last night, so now they light their bonfires in the hopes he will come and sit with them on the beach and tell stories of growing up in Baiting Hollow, traveling to Alaska and all around the world. Bobby said the Captain told him he would try to come back this weekend to see us.

Barbara said, "He sounds like the ancient Irish storytellers. They walked all over Ireland, traveling from town to town. Families hoped the storyteller would choose their home to come to. He was considered the bearer of old lore and given great hospitality: a hearty dinner, warm fire, dry clothes, and a bed for the night."

Barbara continued, "The family would sit around the fireplace after dinner with the storyteller seated in a large chair by the fire. When he was ready, he would tell stories about the beginning of time when volcanoes rose from the sea and red molten lava bubbled out of the earth to form the land now called Ireland. He told the great myths, stories of Saint Patrick, and stories of fairies and banshees. He told of seamen lost to storms, sea creatures, dragons, whirlpools, and volcanic eruptions. Families heard stories of silkies and mermaids, how captains were lured by their beauty and their song, and how their ships would become wrecked on the rocky outcrops of the untamed Irish coast."

Brigid listened and wondered if Kevin O'Connell ever told the story he shared with her one night over fifty years ago about their being descendents of the mermaid, Abigail. Brigid remembered the summer of 1960 as an enchanted time. She knew the summer of 2011 would also prove to be a time of enchantment.

"I can't believe we're going home tomorrow," said Barbara. "Even though it has been a wonderful two weeks, I wish we were staying one more week." Although no one commented, Barbara knew her sister and aunt felt the same way.

Barbara, Brigid, and Aunt Clare watched the children running up and down the night beach playing and giggling. In the darkness they saw bonfires die out and neighbors walk back to their bungalows.

The beach was empty now. The only sounds were the waves on the shore. Amid the silent stillness, Aunt Clare said, "I think I hear footsteps in the sand." Next thing they knew the dark figure of a man was walking toward them, up and over the sand dune, and through the beach grass. Barbara gasped.

"Good evening, ladies," said a familiar voice. As he walked into the porch light, Aunt Clare, Barbara, and Brigid recognized him right away. It was Kevin O'Connell. He stepped onto the deck and gave everyone a hug. "Good to see you," Kevin said.

"And, it's good to see you," Aunt Clare replied.

"Here, come sit down," Barbara said as she pulled a chair from the side of the bungalow.

Kevin had a tanned face, blue eyes, and a short grey-brown beard. He was carrying his camera, a photo album, and a gift of Alaskan haddock for them.

"We're so glad you came to visit tonight," Brigid said and asked, "Did you visit the families around the five bonfires, too?"

"Oh, yes, every one of them. I love seeing old friends and telling the stories and tall tales I've heard on my travels. It's great to have the title, *storyteller*," Kevin said with a smile. "I saw Bobbie and Marcy Edwards last night."

Aunt Clare said, "Yes, they told us. We were sorry we missed you."

"I'm sorry I missed you, too, but glad to see you tonight," he answered. "I took a trip to Alaska the first three weeks of July, stayed at the Tanaku Lodge, and fished every day. I brought you some Alaskan haddock I caught. The fishing boat and lodge cleans, cuts, and freezes all the fish caught. I also brought some photographs of the lodge, people, and nature to show you if you'd like to look at them."

Everyone thanked him for the Alaskan haddock and agreed they would love to see his pictures. Aunt Clare suggested they go inside where the light is better for looking at pictures. So, they did.

Kevin shared pictures he took from the fishing boat of whales, seal, eagles, and other fishermen. He had pictures of the seacoast, icebergs, and the lodge. Kevin said he was having a photo art show in Wading River next year.

Barbara said, "Let us know when and where it will be. We'd love to come."

Then Kevin shared photographs of marshes, creeks, and inlets around Long Island Sound. Amazing images of heron, egrets, geese, swans, sea grass, giant ice age stones, sand dunes, drift wood, sun, sky and beach. He told about going to Orient Point one night last December. "The weather man had predicted a full moon," Kevin explained. "So, I packed my jeep, put my camera around my neck, and trudged through the mud and marsh at Orient Point for a perfect picture. I wanted to capture the moonlight on the water."

"After a few hours, I started to drive home in my jeep. I was heading north on Twomey Avenue approaching the Twomey farmhouse and thought I saw a light flickering in the old maple tree on the north lawn."

"My mother planted that tree when I was a little girl," Aunt Clare said, "When we moved to East Islip, Uncle David gave me a seedling from that tree. I would sit at my desk by my upstairs window and could see right into its canopy. Well, last summer a drunk driver crashed into it. I had to have it removed. I do miss it being in my front yard. So, Kevin, what was flickering in the tree?"

Kevin continued, "I drove up to the edge of the yard, turned off the jeep, and walked over to the tree. As the light appeared, it took the form of an old woman ghost."

Barbara and Brigid gasped, "Oh, my!"

Aunt Clare just smiled.

Kevin pointed to Barbara and Brigid teasing, "Oh, I remember your stories of the Twomey ghosts and banshee, but this was really scary. I hollered out to the ghost, 'Hello. Who are you? What are you doing up there?' and the light went out. I waited and watched for five or ten minutes and then decided to leave."

"As I turned to walk away I saw the light and heard a soft frail voice say, 'Wait. Please don't go.'"

"I slowly turned and to my surprise I was looking into the dark hollow eyes of the ghost. I froze. I couldn't say a word. I always liked listening to your stories about the Twomey ghosts and banshee, but I never really believed them. Now, there she was, and I knew no one but you ladies would believe me."

"Then, what happened?" Brigid asked.

"In the cold darkness of that December night, it started to snow. One little snowflake hit my nose, another touched my cheek, and before I knew it snow filled the sky and started coating the ground. It was beautiful," Kevin paused to remember.

"What about the banshee?" Barbara coaxed Kevin.

"O.K.," Kevin continued. "The light from the ghost came and then went like the beating of a heart. When the ghost spoke, soft silver light haloed her figure."

"'I am the Twomey banshee. My name is Maeve Marion. You don't have to be afraid of me. I came to Long Island from Ireland with John and Elizabeth Twomey when they immigrated here during the potato famine in Ireland around 1860. John later traveled back to Ireland to bring his parents, John and Nancy Twomey, to live with them on Long Island. I have watched over the Twomey clan on their first farm in Baiting Hollow, then here on Twomey Avenue in Calverton for over 150 years, and for several hundred years before that in Ireland. If I can foresee any member of the family might be in danger, I let out a blood curdling wail. The wail alarms the family to come to help their relative.'"

"Why are you out here tonight?"

"'I will tell you. Kevin O'Connell, you have been a friend, like family, to all the Twomey relatives. I have watched you photograph Baiting Hollow and the seacoast of Long Island, capturing on film the beauty of this area. When people see, really see, the beauty in nature and appreciate the delicate balance of air, sea, land, and animal life, they will be more likely to value and protect it.'"

"'Kevin, I watched you tonight and knew you would be driving past the Twomey farmhouse. I wanted to tell you, so you could warn Barbara, daughter of Lillian Twomey, granddaughter of David and Margaret Kaelin Twomey, and great granddaughter of John and Elizabeth Twomey that she will have choices to make in the near future. Barbara loves Calverton, Long Island, and the Twomey farmhouse. It will be up to her to save the family home for future generations of Twomey descendents now scattered all over the United States.'"

"I explained that I was now confused, 'I don't understand. Please tell me what is happening? What do you see? And, what do you want Barbara to do?'"

"The banshee disappeared from sight. The snow was falling steadily now as I stood shivering in front of your Grandma Twomey's maple tree. I looked up in the snow filled night sky and waited."

"'Kevin, come up here and sit with me,' the banshee ordered. I looked up and once again saw the old woman ghost in the split of the limbs about six feet off the ground and decided to join her."

"'Kevin, look in the living room windows of the family home. What do you see?' The banshee raised her arm and pointed toward the living room windows. A light streamed from her finger across the snow covered lawn, over the front porch, and lit up the living room."

"The light coming from the family home made it look like a Thomas Kinkaid Christmas painting. There was a large Christmas tree by the front window, and, yes, Barbara and Brigid were decorating the tree," explained Kevin.

"Then I asked the banshee, 'What happened? Am I dreaming or in a trance? I'm leaving,' I said as I started to climb down the tree."

"'Please, don't go,' Maeve Marion implored. 'Stay, listen, and understand. I have rushed the story. I told you I have watched over the Twomeys for over 400 years in Ireland and here. I always felt like an important part of the family. I always felt appreciated and needed. Grandma Twomey left in her will that the house and I would remain in the family as long as a Twomey descendent lived here. Well, the house has been sold. I am no longer needed. So, I'm dissolving into the atmosphere, my light flickering on and off. I know Barbara wants to live here. If she buys the family home, I will stay here with her. Barbara loves her family and has proven she would do anything for her family and friends. I would help her protect the Twomey home, history, and family.'"

"So, I paused and sat back down in the tree. The banshee put her bony arm around my shoulder, pointed through the dark snowy evening and said, 'Look, Kevin. Look in the windows of the Twomey farmhouse. What do you see?' The stream of light from the old banshee once again lit up the farmhouse."

****

"Are there anymore decorations in the attic, Brigid?" Barbara *asked hanging the last ornament on their Christmas tree.*

"I think there are garlands, window lights, and a manger still up there," Brigid recalled. "Do you want me to get them?"

"No, I'll get them. You better check on the dinner," Barbara answered. Then she went up the staircase to the attic to retrieve the final box of Christmas decorations.

Brigid headed to the kitchen through the dining room and paused to admire the dining room table. Her mother's Christmas tablecloth, grandmother's bone china trimmed in gold (a gift to her from Uncle Al Meyer), silverware, and an advent wreath with three purple and one pink advent candles. It was beautiful and ready for Christmas Day dinner.

Walking into the kitchen she saw the large pot on the stove boiling over. She ran to take the lid off just in time. The chili had been simmering all afternoon. She stirred the chili and turned the heat down just as the timer rang. Her rolls were done and ready to come out of the oven. Brigid had used Aunt Mame's recipe and knew they would be delicious with the chili. Brigid brushed a little melted butter on top of the rolls and set them on the counter to cool.

Barbara had set the kitchen table with Aunt Mame's red floral trimmed dishes and a pretty red and white plaid tablecloth. Brigid smiled and straightened the corner of the tablecloth.

Brigid met Barbara in the living room and helped set up the manger on the table by the stairs. Barbara looked out the window and said, "Boy, the snow is really coming down. Let's turn on the television and see how the road conditions are."

"Blizzard conditions, telephone wires are down, no electricity in most Suffolk county communities...Police are asking people to stay off the roads," the weatherman reported.

"Oh no. Now, Aunt Clare, Uncle Bud, Aunt Jerry, Uncle Harry, Eddie, Amy, Kelly, James, Isabella, David, and Dave can't come here. We haven't heard from them because they can't call, text, or email us," Barbara said realizing for the first time how terrible it was outside.

"Barbara, we're alright. We do have electricity, heat, a gas stove for cooking, and water," Brigid said trying to look for some good in the situation they found themselves in. Maybe they will come tomorrow."

Barbara walked over to the stable and looked at the Baby Jesus, Mary, and Joseph. She turned toward Brigid and said, "Yes, all is well. It is Christmas Eve."

Barbara and Brigid hung a garland of evergreens around the banister, put candles in the windows, watered the poinsettias, and put all the boxes back in the attic.

While they were in the attic they were surprised to hear knocking at the back kitchen door and then knocking at the front door. "Who could be here?" Barbara asked.

They came down the stairs, and Brigid ran to answer the kitchen door. Barbara started to open the front door. As she turned the door knob, a gust of snow blinded her vision. At the same time, the wind pushed the door open, and it hit her in the face.

She recovered from the bang on the head and was surprised to see her mother, Lillian, and her father, Alfred, standing there. They hugged, kissed, and asked where Brigid was. Barbara was in shock.

"Oh, there she is with Eddie," Mom said with delight. "They are coming through the dining room now." Mom and Dad gave Brigid and Eddie hugs and kisses, too.

Barbara looked at Brigid in disbelief. They both shrugged their shoulders, "Oh, well."

Barbara smiled and whispered, "I don't know what's happening, so let's just enjoy ourselves." Brigid nodded.

"Your home looks beautiful," Daddy said. "It's been a long trip. I could really use a cup of coffee."

"I'll get it," Brigid said and went into the kitchen.

Barbara invited her father and brother to sit on the couch and enjoy the tree with her.

Walking into the kitchen Brigid saw her mother stirring the chili. "Oh, Brigid, did you make this? It's delicious. I always liked your chili. Oh, homemade rolls, too. You have been busy."

"Thank you, Mom," Brigid said smiling and hugging her mother again. "Daddy and Eddie want a cup of coffee. Would you like one too?"

"Yes, thank you. That would be fine," said Lillian. "Can I do anything to help you?"

"The sugar bowl and pitcher are on the tray over on the counter. Would you get five coffee mugs and the cream from the refrigerator? Please put some cream in the pitcher and bring the tray into the living room. I'll bring the coffee pot," Brigid suggested.

Entering the living room, Brigid saw Eddie was coming down the stairs. He smiled at her. He looked so handsome. She knew they would have a wonderful evening.

Mom, Dad, Eddie, Barbara, and Brigid reminisced while looking at the old Christmas photo album. After dinner they enjoyed one more cup of coffee and Christmas cookies in the living room. Lillian said, "We are home again."

Alfred answered, "Yes, we are."

Barbara told everyone about running into the owners of the farmhouse on the beach last summer and hearing they might sell. They gave her a tour of the house that same day. At that time she wasn't sure how it would happen. In October they phoned her ready to sell. They met, agreed on the price, had an inspection and closing, and she moved in at the end of the University's fall semester. "On December 20th, Rocky, Matt, Maggie, Brigid, Kelly, Amy, James, and Dave helped me move and set up. We decided to have Christmas here this year. But, I guess the blizzard changed their plans," Barbara explained.

As Lillian started to speak, "We're so proud of you, Barbara…" There was a knock at the back door, and the lobby door opened. They could hear hearty laughter and talking. Eddie said he would see what was going on.

Brigid, Barbara, Mom, and Dad heard Eddie's laughter and his greeting the Christmas Eve guests. Brigid asked, "Do you think they are carolers?"

Barbara shook her head, "No, we didn't hear any singing outside. Carolers usually come to the front lawn and sing until someone opens the door to welcome them in for warmth and refreshments."

They could hear Eddie in the kitchen say, "Come on in. I'll take your coats."

Daddy stood up and said, "Stay here. I'll have a look."

The next thing they heard their father call from the kitchen, "Lillian, Barbara, Brigid come here!"

Lillian led Barbara and Brigid through the dining room. The kitchen was full of relatives. Over Lillian's shoulder, Brigid saw the relatives and called to Barbara saying, "Barbara, I see Aunt Mame, Uncle David, Aunt

Alice and Uncle Lyndon, Uncle Johnny and Aunt Helen, Uncle Joe and Aunt Betty, Aunt Peggy and Uncle Vernon, Little Loretta, Uncle Chris and Aunt Betty, Aunt Agatha and Uncle Al, Uncle Frank, and I think Grandma and Grandpa Twomey!"

When Barbara reached the door to the kitchen, she was that surprised to see her mother, Lillian, hugging her mother and father. The room was filled with relatives' talking, hugging, laughing, and kissing. It was a grand reunion.

Barbara started to feel light-headed. She felt sad that the storm had delayed the arrival of Uncle Bud, Aunt Clare, Aunt Jerry, Uncle Harry, Amy, Kelly, James, Isabella, David, and Dave. The room started to spin, Barbara fainted, and she slammed her head on the corner of the kitchen counter and then fell on the floor.

****

"Do you know what happened then?" Kevin asked.

"No, tell us what happened," Barbara said.

"Nothing," Kevin said and folded his arms in front of himself.

"What do you mean nothing?" Barbara asked.

"The lights went out. The vision was gone. I felt like an old fool sitting in the old maple tree. Then I noticed the first light of dawn. I was ready to go home," Kevin explained.

"What does it mean?" Barbara asked.

Aunt Clare spoke up, "It means you have hopes and dreams. You have family and friends who will always love you. You have choices. Pray to your relatives. Tell them about your hopes and dreams. They are always with you. It means anything is possible."

"It means Kevin O'Connell is a great storyteller," Brigid added with a smile.

Out of the silence of the moment, Barbara exclaimed, "Oh my! It's dawn. There's the first light on the eastern horizon."

Kevin took a deep breath, stood up, and said, "Well, it's been nice visiting with you. I better get going. How long will you be staying?"

"We're going home tomorrow," Brigid explained. "Thank you for visiting and sharing your pictures and stories. Thank you for bringing us Alaskan haddock. It's so good to see you again."

Kevin gave Aunt Clare, Barbara, and Brigid hugs and kisses. They all walked outside to the beach road together and waved to him as he walked away and got in his jeep. He waved back and just as he drove up Edward's Avenue the sun came up.

"Good morning!" Bobby Edwards called from the front porch of his family bungalow. "I thought you were going home today."

Aunt Clare waved, smiled, and walked over to talk with Bobby, her childhood friend, and Marcy. Barbara and Brigid waved and promised to come over when they were leaving. They went back into their bungalow for a hot cup of coffee. Aunt Clare joined them, and they all started to pack and clean. Around 11:00 AM, they walked out onto the deck, and Barbara locked the bungalow door. They stopped to say good-bye to Bobby and Marcy. Aunt Clare headed to her home in East Islip, and Barbara and Brigid headed home to Connecticut.

****

Printed in the United States
By Bookmasters